A Lil' Somethin' on the Side

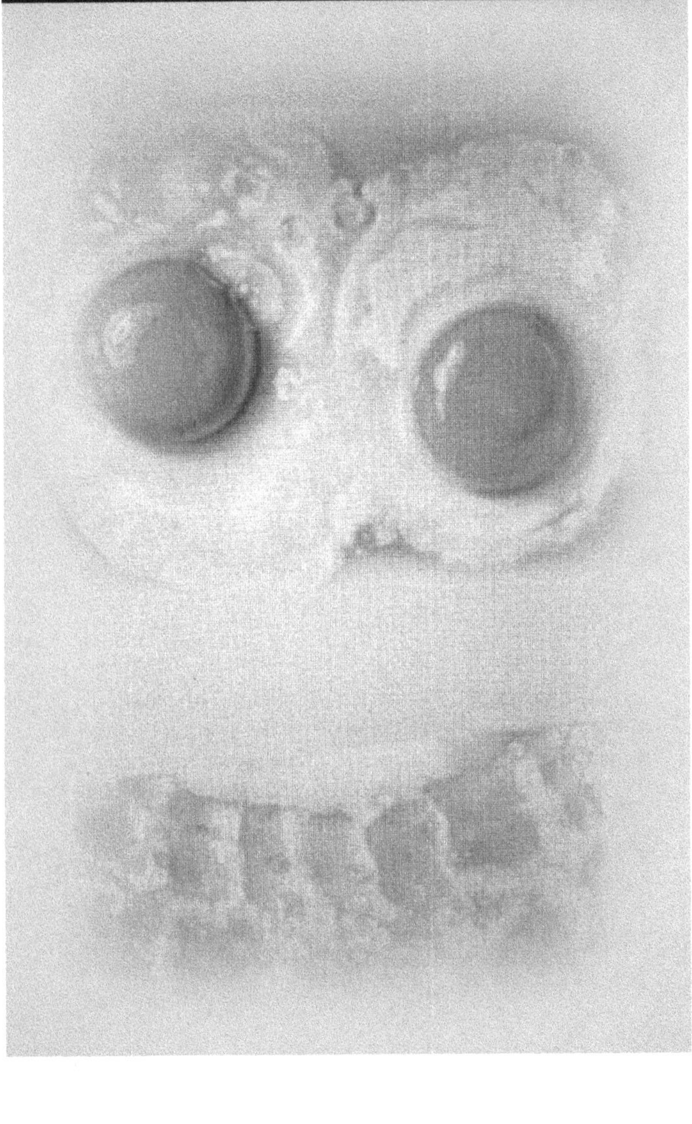

Printed in the United States of America

First Edition

BISAC Fiction / Motivational & Inspirational

10 9 8 7 6 5 4 3 2 1

ACKNOWLEDGMENTS

I would like to thank my parents for always encouraging my creativity and believing in me. I am surrounded and supported in every way by parents: Forrest and Terry, Sharyn and Paul, and Nancy and Gordon. I could not have taken the time that it takes to write, nor all of the trips I venture out on to inspire me, if not for this gang! I want to thank my kids for laughing me through all of it!

Brian—my Bri Guy—I could never have this life without your ever-ending support! Plus, your extra set of eyes and ears have been a plus as well! You are the best computer guy I know and I am glad to always keep you busy fixing my messes with my laptop(s)! You make a wonderful go-to partner for tea and coffee breaks, I must add!

I want to give special thanks and props to Chris, without you books would take twice or three times as long. Whenever I take time doubting what I have, you are the first to remind me that I have something worthy of going forward. You always get first full read though because I trust you and value your input. Your encouragement sparks my creativity! Lori and Siobhan—we have unique stories to how we met. No coincidence, just being brought together as we were always supposed to be! Julia, my friend from always, still here a text away to help out. I cannot thank you ladies enough for your time in reading my work and for your suggestions to make these projects better.

I borrowed some personalities from the past to develop these characters. People who I worked in an office with back when I was counseling regularly, made strong impressions on me for different reasons. Those years were a special moment in time for me and just borrowing a name or quirky line some of them used to say, would bring a big smile to my face all of these years later. To "My Colleen" especially—what I wouldn't give for one more day with you as my secretary!

My coffee ladies, you listen week after week over numerous cups of coffee to the next story lines, the publishing saga, the book signing plans and more! You listen to me read chapters, and for some of you, even whole books! I treasure each of you--Annie, Libby, Linda, Pam, Paula, and Robin.

To Elk Creek Vineyards for an enticing, peaceful setting for writing.

To Nick and Pam for the perfect setting to prepare my mind for writing and to finish the book in a tropical paradise that calmed and restored my soul.

To Crossroads Church for always helping keep my eyes above the waves...

Capturing Memories by Siobhan Eileen for headshots this year for my covers.

I want to mention just a few of the people that have lifted me in other ways specifically during the time of writing this particular book, whether it be words, hugs, random texts, sunrises, or sending positive energy in their own special way. Steve, Lianne, Manda, Krista, Patty, Suzannah, Jeff, Kim, Gail, Mary, Larry, Michelle, Tander, and a very special person in my life, Mike!

"Hi! I'm Sunnie, and you're watching the Sunny Side Up segment brought to you today by Add-An-Egg—yummy, tasty egg substitute. A great way to start your day sunny side up!"

Thank you for tuning in this morning. Today I will be talking to you about finding your inner peace, every day. I know that you probably think that you are too busy to find this 'state of mind' every day, but I am going to share with you how to do this by using some simple steps, that will take just three to five minutes of your day. The first thing you can do toward finding your inner peace is to identify the place in your home where you are most peaceful. For me, that looks like the cleanest room in the house which varies by day," I deliver the line, winking into the camera. "I like to do this first thing in the morning to start my day. I take a deep breath, telling myself to take in the new day with my breath in, and then let go of everything from yesterday with my breath out. Once I have completed that breathing technique effectively three times, I declare out loud, a few of the items I would like to accomplish in the day ahead. This allows me an attitude of gratitude to recognize that I am given this day to be productive, no matter how great or small my tasks are for this particular day. This next part is very individual so you should try-on some of the different ways to find what is best for you. I personally like to either toast my coffee mug into the air or give myself a nice big smile in the mirror and say, "I've got this!" no matter what IT may be for the day ahead. I somehow just know that it will be a great day starting Sunny Side Up! Thank you for watching."

"Okay. CUT! Sunnie, head to wardrobe, and then as soon as you get changed, get to Studio 3 to film the new promo of your segment. And Sunnie, don't be late to the meeting. Representatives from Add-An-Egg will be there to discuss how their product is changing."

"Let me guess…NO egg, at all" I hear from the direction of a camera operator who delivers the sarcastic joke under his breath with a smirk. Though no one else reacts much, I smile, maybe a little bigger than I should in front of the crew. *He's cute and a sense of humor!*

"Got it! I will be there, heading to wardrobe now," I say, following orders.

Walking down the hall at the best pace my heels will allow, I remember the deep breaths I had just taken with my audience out there. So much for the calmness that those deep breaths can bring! You have to find inner peace in minutes because someone is always going to try to steal it in seconds! Now THAT is what I should tell my audience!

Again following orders, I send the first, of many I am afraid, promotional tweets.

Tweet: sunnie@sunnysideup Watch for promo video filmed today. Will sneak a preview to all my fans who re-tweet #sunnysideup

"Good morning, Sunnie," I am greeted by Sam as I climb into the hair and make-up chair. "I saw your tweet about the promo video last night. How did you see the video clip already?"

"I didn't, but they asked me to get the buzz started. When they tell me to leak it out a little, I am guessing that about 2,576 followers will do," I say with a giggle of excitement. *This happened quickly!*

"I would say that's a start," Sam says while applying some primer to what is called the five points on my face.

"I don't really get caught up in all this following and re-tweeting that they make me do as part of the job. Well…until I did start caring, like this morning when I saw my first mean tweet. Seriously, who takes the time to put a damper on a sunny day? I am supposed to be positive, bright, making people's days sunnier and someone has to knock that? Who says you can't change someone's life 3 minutes at a time? Well, you can! I listen to what I say every day, and I see differences all the time!"

"Hold still," Sam says rubbing the crème evenly into my skin.

"I am getting so worked up over this. It is ridiculous! I don't want to talk about this or think about it anymore!"

"I know you don't want to talk about it but what, may I ask, did the 'mean tweet' say?"

"It said that…my hair looks yellow," I say, tapering off at the end, embarrassed to have to say it at all.

"What?"

"That my hair looks yellow!" I repeat.

"C'mon" smirking, "What EXACTLY did it say, Sunnie?"

"It said: Is it just me or is her hair even yellow like the sun? #sunnyyellowrealorfake."

"Is that it?" Sam says laughing.

"Yes, that's it! It's rude, right? My hair is not fake, and it is certainly not yellow."

"I wouldn't worry so much about that. Could be just someone not buying into the whole 'sunny concept'…possibly suggesting the little segments aren't real…you know the whole change your life in three easy steps doesn't come across…as possible…to some people. You have to admit that yourself, right?"

"Is that supposed to make me feel better?"

"Your hair is blonde. Only kids call blondes yellow," Sam says.

"Again I ask you…is that supposed to make me feel better?" I ask in a defeated tone.

Sam spins me around in the chair and points towards the mirror, "Look right there. Do you see a yellow-haired girl or a gorgeous blonde with perfect make-up?"

"Of course you are going to say that for numerous reasons." I see the yellow-haired girl's pout change to a smile.

"Don't doubt yourself, Sunnie. And whatever you do…promise me that you won't read anything about yourself on social media in the mornings before you are on the air again."

"Why? Do you think it will cause me to blow today's segment?" I asked, doubting myself just like Sam told me not to do.

"No, you are better than that. I think that you ARE 'sunny'. It is REAL, not an act. I never fear that you will blow anything actually. But when you come in here with your nose all scrunched up, it is nearly impossible to do infallible make-up! Don't be bringing me down!"

"Oh, I forgot," I smile at both of us in the mirror. "It IS all about you!"

"That's right. And move on now. You are not the only face of today that needs my chair."

During the minutes in my dressing room to review my script for today, complete irony strikes again when I read the title of my segment that they have picked for the day. "Let me show you how to brighten your day by brightening your hair—bring out your natural highlights," I whine into yet another mirror so early in the day. "How could they choose this one…TODAY? Oh, why did I even write this one to begin with!"

After the segment, I retreat to my dressing room for a bit before the meeting. Checking email, deliberately avoiding Facebook and Twitter, and other social media until I get my yellow-topped brain wrapped around how to navigate these. Deleting my Ikea ad and Black and White Market sale notice, so that I am not distracted, I open the next email. Is this directly from the big boss? *Really?*

Attention Sunnie:

Attached is the schedule and format for the department meetings. They are fast-paced so be prepared.

Also, we would like you to increase your use of social media at this time. It is important that your audience feels a connection with you outside of their 3 minutes of viewing. We need to make your viewers think that they are getting to know you more. Without sharing anything you are uncomfortable with, please allow the viewer to become "your friend". Just be that girl they want you to be! Ratings should soar. You are a very likable talent. We expect your following could increase ten-fold almost immediately and that we should expect a good run with this!

Any questions, shoot me an email back, or we can discuss further at the meeting as a group.

Alec

Wow. Just wow. Thanks, boss…Alec. What the—! I have never heard anyone call him anything but Mr. Parker. Well, a few other names, but not A…lec. Oh big boss, Alec, is this your way of making me feel like "your friend"? Maybe next you will be commenting on my Facebook posts. I have some questions alright, Alec! I will address them now!

Mr. Parker,

I received your email regarding social media. I will attempt to lure in viewers by using social media to allow my followers to see me as the likable person that I am or at least the girl they want me to be.

As far as a "good run"??? How about I take a "good run" in the other direction and forget social media and this place too! What would be wrong with giving my audience the 3 minutes of my personality per day that I signed up for?

Thanks for bringing this matter to my attention!

Yeah, so Alec, I do not think that I should send this to you because it is more than obvious that I really do not know how to respond to what exactly you may be saying here.

So am I supposed to thank him that he finds me to be "likable talent" or be offended that he seems to be asking me to be who the viewers want me to be? Oh my goodness, what have I gotten into this time?

I thought that I was chosen for my down to earth, good appealing ideas in the first place. I thought that I was picked for the segment because I am a sunny person capable of making someone's day. I thought that I was "likable" and "talented" and that viewers would like that about me, along with the useful tidbits of information that I would provide. I thought THAT was going to be enough to make ratings soar.

Okay big boss, Alex, now that I have this off my chest I will be able to revise the email, keeping what is good.

Mr. Parker,

I received your email regarding social media.

Sunnie

I re-read this email again, attempting to add content—preferably the type of content that does not cost me my job, nor my integrity. Clearly a sword with more than one edge here. I wish I had a segment already filmed on this topic that I could tune into for help—how to charm your boss and the world at the same time? But wait there's more! You have to stay true to yourself! That's it! That is what I would tell my viewers, YOU have to be true to yourself! And that is what I will tell my good ole buddy Alec. And forget the email, I will tell him in person! That is the way I do things—head on!

"Hi! I'm Sunnie, and you're watching the Sunny Side Up segment brought to you today by Add-An-Egg—yummy, tasty egg substitute. A great way to start your day sunny side up!"

Today I will be talking about how to pack your lunch, and make a healthy drink for your family, good for the whole day! This is the epitome of healthy multi-tasking! I like to keep healthy items like these on hand," I say, holding up a cucumber,

19

"and I think that you are going to want to, as well, when you see how easy this is. Simply cut a side of the peel away from a cucumber length-wise, so that you have a nice long strip of the peel with a bit of the cucumber flesh, drop it right down into your pitcher. Grate a little ginger, putting part of it into the pitcher and part aside to layer into your lunch jar. Cut a lemon into wedges so that you can squeeze and drop them into the water pitcher, saving one sizable squirt for over your lunch jar. In case you missed the previous segment, these glass jars are a nice and safe way to keep your fresh foods. Plus, doesn't it just look pretty! Whatever else you would like to add to your jar lunch is up to you! Only you know what kind of day you will be having! I like to add layers of lettuce, spinach or kale, and other veggies that I happen to have. You can even throw on a layer of sliced boiled eggs for some protein as well. For more about layering your lunch jar, you can go to our website for last week's tips. Don't forget to drink your veggie-infused water all throughout the day. I truly hope that it is a sunny day! Thank you for watching Sunny Side Up."

Gathered around the U-shaped table, I am feeling pretty confident among my peers on the team. A whole new shuffle is invented when Mr. Parker enters the room. I fathom the idea of suddenly changing this dynamic if I were to call out, "Over here, Alec, by me!" I refrain.

"Let's get started," he says conducting the meeting, calling on people's reports before he gets situated in his seat. His lack of eye contact and body language, ruffling through his papers leads me to believe that he could care as much what they were saying as hearing the weather report on a different planet. Upon further observation, I conclude he is the type to easily multitask to the point that he can be aware of everything going on in the universe, possibly even the weather on different planets. A rather sexy quality in a man. I'm impressed!

"Miss Grey? Anything to report?" That brought me back from sexy-man fantasy quickly. I thought I would have a little more time before discussing the social media suggestions he had made in the email.

"Well—" I say in the most professional stalling tone that I could.

Waiting for no pause to end, he moves on, "So I assume that you have seen the email and that we can expect to see a blast in social media buzz about you ASAP. Everyone loves to see what's new."

"Well, about that—" my pause again is interrupted with him moving on.

"In time we can get someone to help with this, if it gets too hard to keep up. See what you can do right away, Miss Grey, using all social media outlets."

I get the feeling that no one interrupts the words, thoughts, or even pauses of Mr. Parker. Where did my buddy "Alec" go? Oh, I get the feeling that I don't have a buddy Alec either. Maybe he is more like Mr. A-lec-to-manipulate-people-into-doing-just-what-I-want-Parker. Figuring this out now could be useful information for me. I will just keep it to myself, not planning on blasting it to social media just yet.

"Hey, Miss Grey, is it? I didn't get a chance to formally meet you yet, but I was part of the crew taping your segment the other day," says a very good-looking person next to me.

"Oh yeah, I remember you…the eggless joke," I smile, as big as I had wanted to when the joke had been made.

"Ha! Crazy that they let some of these sponsors even in the door. Seems pretty contradictory sometimes. Anyway, I'm Mike. It is nice to meet you," he says, extending his hand.

"Sunnie. Sunnie Grey," I say taking his hand on the end of his too-nice-not-to-notice arm.

"Really? Sunnie Grey? And I thought that fake eggs sponsoring your Sunny Side Up segment was contradictory!"

"Oh yeah, I have heard that before…but I look at it like…"

"Oh Mikey…ever thought of WORKING at your workplace?" another guy from the crew calls over before I could explain my contradictory name.

"Gotta go, Miss Sunnie Grey. I will have to hear how you picked your stage name at a later time." He flashes me an amused smile before he joins the crew heading out of the room together.

My mouth remains open, enough to catch rain on my tongue, as I was about to explain that I didn't pick my name. Clearly, it had picked me.

My conversation with my crewman, Mike, did cause me to forget about Mr. Parker's request for a bit. Maybe I could just start blasting social media tomorrow.

"Miss Grey," a voice from behind me that is coming right out of the mouth of Mr. Parker when I spin around, "Please follow Colleen now. She is going to get you set up with an App so that your phone can automatically upload all of your photos to our system as you take them. She can handle picking which ones to post right away. I don't want you to be overwhelmed." He keeps moving right out the door before I can say, YOU expect that every photo I take should be immediately seen by someone else so that THEY may decide which to post, AND YOU DON'T THINK that would OVERWHELM ME???

"Mr. Parker must really want to keep you around. I have never seen him, hmmm…think so creatively just to have someone 'not be overwhelmed'. C'mon, follow me." This comes from the voice that must be Colleen, my new "easy" button.

"Sure," I say following her down the hall trying to remember that this isn't her fault. I wonder if SHE also ever contemplates how she got here, following Mr. Parker's orders.

"Hand over your phone and your privacy too, ha-ha!" Colleen laughs a little more, though her joke is not funny in the least.

"Maybe I should try to do it myself for a while and if it gets to be too much, I could let you know, or let Mr. Parker know, and then, make a plan," I say hesitantly, but still holding on to my phone for the chance this idea would go away.

"Are you kidding me? When Alec, I mean when Mr. Parker gets a plan, it is already in motion. You are better to move in the same direction the motion is traveling if you know what I mean." Without much subtlety, Colleen peels my fingers off of my phone and opens my App store as if she has controlled my phone for longer than phones have been smart. I decided it would be smart of me to play along at this point. Maybe I can even out-smart this, I think.

I leave with my smartphone in hand, smart enough to not take any pictures that I wouldn't want to chance being posted. HA! When do the "Brilliant Phones" come out? I will be waiting! In the meantime, I will continue to post just a little to wet the taste buds, but not enough to reveal my flavor! Brilliant, I think.

What in the world did Colleen do to my phone? It is buzzing and blinking to alert me continuously before I even get out of the building. I make a decision to wait to check it at home on the computer so I can focus better. I know that I am in denial and that very soon I am going to need to become one of those people who check their Facebook page every day or even multiple times a day, but for now I like waiting for the message sent to me from Facebook, reminding me that I haven't posted anything in a while. I love when it tells me what I have missed while I have been out living my life instead of documenting it! *Here's what has been happening while you have been away, Sunnie.* I think, oh yeah Mr. Facebook, you will never know what's been happening while I was away! I crank up the car radio now overshadowing the phone buzzing to the point I have forgotten its hum, while I'm humming along to the lyrics until the chorus comes back around. Then I belt out the words without a care in the world about social media! I don't need to explain myself to anyone. I don't need to pump up my following until everyone knows my name. I don't even need to explain my name. It's coming up. I just need to, sing it with me…how great is our God…and all will see how great, how great is our God…I sing pulling into my spot. When I park, I resist taking a selfie in my happy state, not knowing how great I look to anyone, except God, at the moment. I will protect this beautiful moment from leaking to the media. I have the hang of this already!

Squeezing lemon into my cucumber green tea, I only wish I squirted some into my eye so that I did not have to see that 893 people LIKE my photo in the past 27 minutes. Wait—I didn't know that I had that many friends? Oh okay, more than 27 shares in 27 minutes will do that sort of thing! Let's see if I LIKE my photo? I click to see myself along with my book club friends in swimsuits on a boat. This is when I start an extremely loud conversation with my computer. "Who would post this photo? Who would tag me in this photo? How did—wait—it shows that I am the one who actually posted this photo? This picture is on my phone, but I would never share it. My phone, my phone...Colleen—Oh, dear God."

At first I only feel exposed, knowing that more than half of my breasts are making their debut on the internet, but later I just feel sad. I see some text messages from friends in the picture with me. I don't read them, not until I can get my head together and send an apologetic explanation of how this happened. I feel robbed of more than my right to decide how much boob to share with who. I feel stripped of a special day—a day in which my friends and I had planned and executed the way we had wanted to do it, with just our little group who loved and trusted each other, just like the characters in the book had.

Our book club book of the month had taken place at George Lake. Though usually we take turns rotating to each of our houses to discuss our book club book, this time we finished the book near the end of summer and wanted to do something more special. We rented a little cottage on the lake, but not just on any lake. We rented a place on the exact lake in the book. Furthermore, we didn't just discuss the book; we acted out the characters throughout the time we were there. I got to play the part of the blonde character with the big boobs pouring out of a red bikini top! We had a rented pontoon, we had drinks, and we had a lovely time with those characters, and with each other. I really liked that day. And now I find out that other people LIKE it too. Those people just don't know the story behind it, but it doesn't seem to stop them from SHARING the photo! They probably just see a yellow-haired girl in a red suit, barely in a red suit.

I open a bottle of red wine and close my laptop. I need to relax and get some sleep before I can find a solution to make myself and Mr. Parker content. With my first sip from my wine glass, I wish I were back drinking from plastic, on that boat with my friends. I felt so pretty and so confident, just like the character in the book—a woman who really knew herself.

Things always look better in the morning, my dear friend always tells me. That is, if she still wants to talk to me at all. I sleep it off and return to the station in the morning.

It is funny to me that when ironic occurrences become so frequent, the irony is lost in its predictability. I sit in my dressing room chair moments before my segment, rehearsing my lines, of how to get ready for swimsuit season in three simple steps. I wonder who picked this one for today!

But I will get through it. I am Sunnie. It is real, and I will not doubt myself through this. Even covered by a rather conservative gray suit today, this yellow-haired girl in a red swimsuit is learning something new every day in this business.

Hopefully the viewers out there like this segment, from business suit to swimsuit. The topic sure wasn't lost on the filming crew, I could tell. "Well hello, Miss Grey," says a voice that followed me off the set and into the hallway.

"Hi Mike," I smile. "Are you referring to the suit or my name? Because I told you that you could call me Sunnie."

"The suit." Mike keeps on walking without an ending to the conversation he started. I had planned to explain to him about the name.

I pass a few others in the hall, seemingly eyeing me up and down. I like this place, though; everyone is busy. I think I could handle a longer conversation with some of the crew, but I like that the lack of time stretches out the rate we get to know each other. Keeps things simpler as well, people seem too busy to read into anyone else's business. Everyone seems just to know their place. Except for me.

I crash into Mr. Parker's arms as I round the corner. Oh my goodness, does he smell good.

"Well Miss Grey, you certainly smell nice. Too bad our viewers can't know this through the tube to go with their visual!" he smiles while rubbing his hands up and down my arms, as if it were perfectly normal to crash into each other and converse while still embraced.

"Yes, too bad. I am sure that will be invented next with how fast things are happening," I quickly add, "I meant with the internet, and apps, and inventions, and—" when I realize how dumb I must sound to my boss. I didn't want him to think I was accusing him of anything moving along too fast. I just really want him to see that I am good at my job.

"You know, Sunnie, you are really doing a good job!" More arm rubbing, but he is saying the right thing.

"Thank You, Mr. Parker. I love my job!" I reply, accepting the compliment.

"Sunnie, you have already given us more than we thought we were getting from you. And Sunnie, please, you can call me Alec when we are like this.

I sure like how you use everything you have to sell this segment. You are an amazing find!" His smile was brilliant, his words…not so much.

Finally, out of the unexpected conversational embrace, I walk down the hall with a fake, plastered smile to everyone I pass, while my what-the-hell-just-happened smile gladly hid behind it.

The words "you are an amazing find" play over in my head. I wish he could have just stopped at "you are doing such a good job"! Regardless, I decide to keep playing it to avoid reading into Mr. A-lec-how-you-use-everything-you-have-to-sell-the-segment-Parker's behavior.

"Hi! I'm Sunnie, and you're watching the Sunny Side Up segment brought to you today by Add-An-Egg—yummy, tasty egg substitute. A great way to start your day sunny side up!"

Thank you for tuning in this morning. I want to ask—" I lean in toward the camera, "how's your mood today? Would you like to know some simple ways to help improve it? Today I am going to share with you some new and easy to use tools to feel happier by using something you probably already have in your hand." I pull up a fake phone prop for the segment. "Yes—your phone—can improve your mood! Ignore those calls and texts coming in for just a few minutes and use one of the many mood Apps available. There are quite a few out there to choose from so that you can find the app that best…suits your mood. Some of these mood-tracking apps work by asking you a series of questions about your life and suggesting tips for happiness that have been recommended by psychologists. And here's something else to make you happy…a lot of these apps are free! In addition to boosting your happiness, some of these apps give reminder notifications to reduce stress and teach you how to live more carefree. I do plan to try some of these apps, but I wouldn't get rid of your To-Do list just yet, perhaps you can reduce stress by simplifying and shortening your list! Here is mine, if you would like to copy," I wink at the camera. "Just three items on it: 1. Smile. 2. Be grateful. 3. Be happy! Give it a try! My only fear is that if you find out just how simple it is to have happier, sunnier days, I am going to talk myself out of a job! Thanks for watching Sunny Side Up. Have a very sunny day!"

"CUT!"

"Didn't know where she was going with that, feel happier by using something you already have in your hand bit," says one of the crewmen, as if "she" were already out of the room.

I have two choices here – I can walk out without acknowledging hearing the comment and all the laughter around it, or I can ask for some clarification, which with my mouth's way of twisting up words, could make it worse. Suddenly I realize that I have another, more Sunnie, option and turn back around calling out.

"Hope that comment helps to improve your mood, gentlemen! Have a sunny day!" I call, then walk right out on that note.

"Hey wait up." I don't even have to turn around to know that it's Mike. "Sunnie, this less than two-minute walk seems to improve my mood daily," I smile up at him.

"Really, well then, keep the habit!" I say, with my smile engaged until he has ducked off and no longer looking. Actually, my amused smile continues as I walk. *I am definitely in a good mood!*

"Hi! I'm Sunnie, and you're watching the Sunny Side Up segment brought to you today by Add-An-Egg—yummy, tasty egg substitute. A great way to start your day sunny side up!"

Thank you for tuning in this morning. Today we will be talking about a simple way for a busy woman to get out of the door faster! And it gets better! This simple trick can get you out of the house quicker without losing anything, including your mind! Two words: Purse Dump. You can find one of these simple storage containers anywhere. This specific one that I have here comes from IKEA. Anyone else saying FIELD TRIP about now? I like this particular one because it can be mounted to the wall. It is also just wide enough to make a nice "Purse Dump" station for me to use as I leave the house. Anyone else go through this…two minutes away from exiting your house you realize: Oh I really need to switch purses? Simply take your current purse over to the Purse Dump and do exactly that—dump." Demonstrating as I speak, I have no fear of sounding the least bit cheesy with this idea because of how much I believe in it. "Bring over the new purse that you will be switching into and begin to load it, picking out the obvious items you will need. This way you can leave all of those receipts and business cards that you have collected in the bottom of your purse right there in the Purse Dump, to go through at another time. Yes, ladies, this saves time! And your peace of mind. You will lose neither! There is another bonus as well when you return after the long day; you won't find a bunch of your belongings in a pile on your bed. You can simply use your bed as it is intended!" Winking right into the camera leaving it to the audience to decide what exactly Sunnie uses her bed for! Perfect!

"Cut," someone from the crew calls out.

"Nice work, Sunnie!" Steven, the new set manager, says to me in front of everyone, "I think you could sell any idea to anyone." Good thing you feel that way since the parenting segment, which I have no idea why I agreed to write, is coming up this week.

"Thanks," I simply reply, heading out to my dressing room.

"Wait up," a familiar voice catches up to me, though I hide how thrilled I am that it did.

"So is that where my number is?" he asks.

"What are you talking about, Mike, where your number—? What are you talking about?" totally confused, I reply.

"Whoa girl, too many questions," he smiles and makes me wait. Really.

"You asked the question. About your number?" I say, still very puzzled.

"Oh, you want my number? Okay, here it is." He slips me a tiny paper and firm touch closing my fingers around it. "Put this one in your phone rather than your, uh, purse dump; you call it?"

"Why does that sound like you are making fun of me?" I giggle which plays right into his wit once again.

"Oh, never," teasingly mocking he begins again, "Nice work Sunnie. I think you could sell any idea to anyone."

"Oh stop!" Without an ounce of hesitation, I wrap both my hands around his arm closest to me, tugging him to quit. Is he flexing or is his arm that big? And why am I still holding onto it as I look up at him? My mouth says, STOP, but nothing about my eyes, nor my hands, are agreeing with the statement.

"I'll stop here actually. Editing calls! Catch you later." Of course, he always goes straight to the editing room right after the shoot. I must have missed my turn down the hallway to wardrobe and my dressing room, but rather than turning around I keep heading toward the break room, as if I meant to, instead of admitting that I was becoming attached to those arms.

No one is in the break room, which means I can have a cup of tea and figure out what just happened back there. Is he just being friendly? It is hard to read people two minutes at a time. I just find him so fascinating. Not to mention I'm fascinated by the fact that I am finding myself thinking about him when he is not around. The way Mike had mocked the sound of Steven's voice complimenting me on selling the audience, should tell me something. I try to make sense of how he didn't seem to like the other director being so hard on me all the time, but neither he does he appear to like this director paying so much attention to me, hmmm. Maybe that does add up? He likes me!

I am interrupted by company, Colleen walks in, "Oh honey, take the jacket off before you get honey all over it." As if I can't drink herbal tea like an adult. "You should have stopped in wardrobe on your way having it re-hung."

Knowing she means well, paired with chamomile, keeps me from a smart-mouthed comment. "You're right. I got a little side-tracked today."

She goes from "bossy Mother" to "enabling Mommy" in two seconds flat, "Here, I'll take it for you." She eases my arm out of the sleeve before I could say that I would do it myself.

"Thanks. Hey Colleen, before you go…uh, never mind." I realize that asking about Mike would only be half as bad as asking about Mike in the public break room where anyone could walk in at any time. I have to laugh to myself of how quickly she had moved on out of the breakroom without prying into my business as to what I may have wanted. People around here are too busy to wait around I suppose. I do like that part!

"Whoa, you are about as HOT as this coffee. Why have we had so many 'bring your shirt to work days' in a row? This is way better." Seriously! This is the guy that was so protective of me when I started here, back when the guys in the break room would hit on me.

"Mike! How is a girl supposed to relax with tea with this kind of chatter in the break room?" Nothing in my tone said that I had minded.

"No complaints here, but I am feeling anything but…RELAXED," Mike says smiling and taking in a deep breath. I believe that I could see the reflection of skin in his eyes.

"Oh, I gave Colleen my jacket to go back to wardrobe. I usually change right after my segment." I know that I was not indecent by any stretch, but I'm a little busty for just a cami, at the workplace none-the-less. Crossing my arms in front of me, I walk straight to my dressing room.

Arriving at work especially early this morning, I am ready to implement my little secret plan. Hoping that it would work and that no one would figure out what I was really up to, I reviewed the plan in my head all the way to the wardrobe room.

"Hey, Jaz. Boss wants me back in the same outfit as yesterday for a little edit to the segment for something they are working on...who knows, right?" I realize I need just to shut up and not over explain a lie.

"No can do! Sorry. That just left out with the other dirties for the cleaners. Had something sticky on the sleeve," she says, reaching under the desk.

"That sucks!" Not meaning to sound so disappointed. "I mean it stinks that I got something on the sleeve." Perhaps honey? "Oh well. I am sure they will work something out."

"Would you like me to call down to see what they want you wearing instead?" she asks sincerely trying to help.

"NO! Don't, don't do that. Don't mention it to anyone. Really." I wish that I didn't sound so desperate. What if she figured out that I made that whole part up so that I could just get the jacket back for the one little second it would take me to handle what I needed to handle.

Pulling her hand up from under the counter where she had been fishing for something, "Were you looking for this? It was in the pocket." Grinning hugely at me as if she were to say "bust-ed" in two syllables.

"Oh yeah. I forget what that is, but I do remember stuffing something in the jacket pocket after the shoot," I say, ignoring the tiny fact that I am blushing at even the site of the tiny paper.

"It's the phone number of one of the camera guys. I looked on the phone list."

I had never given Jaz enough credit. "Oh, that's right. Now I remember. Thanks." I turn to leave quickly.

"Hey Sunnie, wait. Do you need me to let you know when the jacket is back and ready?" Did she really need to rub it in? I shake my head no. "There's no follow-up shoot, right? But there is a Mikey, the camera man," she says with another busted-like smile.

"Apparently…there is. Can we keep this just between us?" I ask, hoping she would respect that.

"Sure, but you should know that Anna was the one to find it. Colleen was still here, so she gave him a quick call to catch him off guard."

"Did it?" Oh my, he is going to hate me.

"Well, if the fact she called didn't catch him off guard, what she said surely would!"

I lean in closer dreading where this is going.

"All she said was 'keep your number, and your hands, out of Sunnie's pockets.'" Jaz's smile grows as she repeated what Colleen had said to Mike. "Pretty funny stuff actually. She wants him for herself, of course!"

"She does?" I can't even picture this, as sexy as she can be, not my Mike.

"Everybody does, right?" Jaz says with a laugh that I can't exactly read.

"Everybody wants Mike?" I ask.

"Of course! He is gorgeous, witty, a gentleman, and a flirt. Have you seen his arms? He is lifting more than cameras; that's for sure. You think any girl here hasn't fantasized about helping him make one of those very special types of movies he makes."

Wow Sunnie, did you think you were the only one to notice? "Wait, what movies?"

"I'm just saying. I don't know what kind of movies Mike makes in his time away from here, but he would probably have the know-how. Not to mention plenty of volunteers!" she smiles seemingly proud of that one.

"I don't know him…that well," I say just to slow this down.

"Well, call the number he gave you, you lucky dog, and that will take care of that!" I start to walk to out. "Wait Sunnie, here is your wardrobe for today. What's your segment? Looks a bit conservative? Even stuffy."

"Thanks. The segment is on how to be a professional woman and still have make-believe play to bond with your toddler," I deliver as if it makes perfect sense.

"So, you don't have any kids, right? Wouldn't it be more believable if you were, I don't know—a Mom?" Jaz seems as much confused as being confrontational.

"Well Ale—, I mean Mr. Parker, has asked me to 'blur the lines' a little. He wants more women to relate to me on all levels. Not just single women without children, he wants the viewers to come from all types of women."

"Oh that just makes perfect sense then, doesn't it?" Jaz smarts off.

"Not really, but the ratings are what make sense to him." Why am I defending this plan? I was as perplexed as Jaz was when they originally sold me on this idea for my image. I resented hitting LIKE to Toddler Time and Once Upon Some Kids, or whatever it's called, just so that my social media fans would start to wonder how old my kids were these days. My kids—the ones I don't have yet. Absurd!

"Just be careful girlie. You don't want Mr. Parker to 'blur the lines' so much that he actually gives you some kiddos!" I wish she paired that with the look of "I'm kidding." I wait for it. She does not.

"You are funny!" pretending that I hadn't ever wondered how far Alec would attempt to blur the professional lines. Also starting to wonder how far I would be willing to look the other way as not to see the lines being blurred, I see myself out of there. I keep walking as if I never heard Jaz call out to me again.

"Well, that jacket is pretty stuffy. Hope Mikey has an imagination to what's underneath it!" Jaz giggles coyly.

Well, guess what Jazzy, Mike doesn't have to have an imagination because little do you know, I sit in the break room in my camisole!

"You didn't seem like yourself, Sunnie. You okay?" Following me out appears to be a new habit that I happen to like of Mike's.

Oh, you mean the wardrobe? It is my sophisticated look. I'm getting my Professional Mom on…whatever that is." I'm not usually so sarcastic either. Where's Sunnie?

"No, I realize that you have no control over the wardrobe chosen for your segments. I meant…your color, your feel, your vibe? You know, what I mean right?"

He notices my color, my feel, my vibe? I am so turned on. Not to mention a little hot in this jacket, that I must keep on! "Oh. I know what you mean. Yeah. I'm fine."

"Look Sunnie, I've got 60 seconds 'til I hit the door of the editing room and you're going to use it to lie to me? Do you know how hard it is to get to know you in two minutes at a time? I run out each day to steal these minutes without anyone making a big deal. Don't waste our time, Sun."

Realizing that he's moving away, and we are already by the editing room door, I hold my tongue. I keep playing the shortened name he called me in my head as he spoke again.

"You are going to have to lie to me some more tomorrow at this point. I won't even have time for a coffee break today, even if the break room has a melon display!" he delivers purposefully and disappears.

There will be no melon break today, Mikey. You are the only one around here worthy of my melons, and it will take more than chamomile to calm this girl down now.

All evening I debate, should I call? He gave his number so he must want me to call. But yet he implied he would be busy all day and just see me tomorrow. Maybe he knew that he had some plans after work. I shouldn't call. He gave me his number two days ago, and I haven't used it. I should call. He may want an explanation of earlier—my color, my feel, my vibe. I should call. Just by the fact that he notices my color, my feel, my vibe—I should call. Okay so that's three 'I should call's in a row, what would stop me from calling now? The knot in my stomach that says NOT to call when I read the comments posted about my segment today.

spicyjams98: Sunnie Grey has children! Who's the daddy? Anyone out there know who it is?

bookbum2c: She used to be seen writing in the local bookstore near my house before she made it big.

FLATTERED they think I have made it big. Uh oh, I read on.

gossipgirl4321: Apparently she has been seen walking out with the big boss at the station. He has so many shows, why would he care for time with such a peon with a 3-minute segment unless she knows three ways to please a boss if you know what I mean.

Suzieque561: You are mean gossipgirl4321. I love the Sunnie segments. That girl is real.

Lizishere14: Agreed! I think she is classy.

Yachtfreak308: I think her lips move and I am suddenly touching myself. Who gives a &@#$ what she is talking about, just keep moving those juicy lips Sunny girl.

I am going to be sick. But of course, I keep reading.

shellyszmiles: I agree with Lizishere14. She is classy! And she is super helpful. My sister and I never miss her segment. We actually try many of the suggestions she makes!

Clarkers: Even if she is not a slutty girl, little miss sunny side up may just find herself bottom side up if Mr. Big-Man Parker wants some of dose eggs! Can't blame a girl for wanting to get to the top.

gossipgirl4321: Yes Clarkers! Exactly! All you haters wouldn't mind if Mr. Parker were walking you to the car and your career was hopping into the next century at light speed.

But I am not! I am not that big, and I am not doing anything to get there faster! Wait, can't I just be known for my segment? Has anyone commented on anything that I actually said?

Sophie549: She's a fake! I am going to stop watching. I liked the trendy fashion ideas, but I didn't know she was a Mom.

I am NOT!!!! I yell at the top of my lungs, waking every baby sleeping on this side of town. But not mine.

Doggydo312: Who cares if she has kids or is the mom of her pets? People please don't bite my head off here, but she does give useful advice. And did anyone see the segment with her pets? Adorable the way she mothers them! I ordered from the company that makes the personalized shirts with a picture of my Chihuahua. Remember the one Sunnie wore on the show?

Finally someone! Finally! I love you. I don't even have a pet, but I love you Doggydo312! Wait, so I get a good comment, and someone seems to understand me and it's a dog lover. I mean I love dogs, but not the way you have to love a dog to use doggydo as your screen name! Well maybe there are already 311 doggydo people I can appeal to, I better not judge the name even though no one hesitates to judge me—my segments, my clothes, my lips, my words, my relationship with my boss, my looks, my—what about me? What about my Sunny personality? Ahhhhh, that makes me remember what Mike had told me he noticed about me, which simply takes all of this other nonsense away.

He judges my color, my feel, my vibe. These people don't GET me at all. I should call him. I should call. *But wait, why would he want to be pulled into this? Why would he have these people presume what he would want out of some time with Sunnie?* The sunny side may not be so bright after all. I won't call. And I certainly won't spend my whole evening reading posts about me from people who don't know me.

Using the hair and makeup station as a confessional, I begin, "Remember weeks ago when you told me what not to do? Well, I did it again last night. I read the posts people write about me."

"So what do people think about their favorite yellow-haired girl these days?" Sam asks so nonchalantly.

"Mixed opinions. But I realize they don't really know me. They are reacting to all the stuff that Mr. Parker makes me do for the show, for the ratings." I wish that it were as simple in my head as I explain it here.

"Alec Parker makes hoop jumpers out of actors…for the ratings. Can it be a coincidence he has eight successful shows on the network? He doesn't need to pay any attention to a 3-minute star, you know?"

"Thanks, Sam. Way to put me in my place." I feel defeated. It is one thing to read it on the internet. It is a whole other thing hearing it from a peer.

"I am trying to put you back in your place. Sunnie, you came in here full of ideas, full of life, full of energy, full of sunshine."

"And now?" I ask as if I don't know.

"And now your makeup is complete. Out of my chair!" Sam says spinning me to the mirror. "Take a look for final approval. You do know that you still have a say here? Alec Parker is mesmerized by his new star! You most definitely have a say."

"Thanks, Sam. I think I needed to hear that…and all of it." Carefully climbing down from the chair, I'm aware of the tightest and shortest skirt I have received from wardrobe yet, that must be about the ratings so that I am not mistaken as a frumpy little mom. Ignoring this fact, I smile to my friendly face of flawless makeup, looking amazing according to the mirror image. I chant all the way down the hall that I STILL HAVE A SAY. That is until I am speechless. Busy getting my sunny side back on while someone else is getting a little of Sunnie's backside on! It felt amazing until I remembered I was in the workplace.

"Sunnie, Sunny girl. You have done it again. One segment and Moms all over town are joining in to see what you do, what you wear, and what you'll say next! Way to go 'little mama'." Which is more confusing, the fact that he is perfectly fine misrepresenting me as a mother, or the fact that he is walking beside me, practically rubbing my ass?

Here is my chance! I didn't practice my chant for nothin'!

I still have a say in this, and I am going to say it now! I have only a couple minutes before my segment. "Mr. Parker. I need to talk to you."

"Oh, I told you, Sunnie, to call me Alec when we are alone! You are a very poor listener. Good thing you are such a good speaker or I couldn't justify having you around," he says with a little spank and rounds the corner returning to the public eye.

Did I just get spanked by my boss? Never in my life did I fathom getting reprimanded for not calling my boss by a first name, privately. But this is not your typical rebuke, as a write up in my file either. No this is more like he flipped the sunny side up like it was over-easy.

"Thank you for tuning into Sunny Side Up today, where YOU can change your life to the sunny side in a matter of minutes," I coach myself through this not to look uncomfortable, though I am. Trying to stick to the exact script, but not look scripted is not easy!

"Before we discuss today's topic, I need to make a minor correction regarding a statement I made about marriage. It was just my opinion that marriage is the best. This network is neither pro-marriage nor pro-single lifestyle. We love all of our viewers the same whether married or not. We even love them the same if they are in a same-sex marriage," I add. Uh-oh! "But…keep in mind, that's my opinion, not that of the local network," I cover. "Moving right into our segment for today, sometimes one of the tiniest things can cause us trouble, but with a few simple steps and you can be free of pesky fruit flies. I know It is rare to count one and then two before it seems that all of the sudden they have taken over your entire kitchen. Well, there are a couple of things I know about these little guys, one they are designed to find fermenting fruit and two, they are persistent. We can be too, in getting rid of the little nuisances. You can use any size glass, but I like to use a brandy snifter—the opening is wide, but the glass is shallow enough to do the trick easily. Yes, the trick that the fruit flies don't have a chance to catch on to!" Wink into the camera! "Pour a little apple cider vinegar into the glass and cover it with a plastic baggie or a piece of clear wrap. Simply secure it with a rubber band. Poking a small hole in the middle will be enough to lure the fruit flies to their…FINAL destination. The fruity aroma is irresistible to these simple-minded creatures so it will not take long to entice a whole infestation to end up inside the vinegar trap. It's that simple! And before you put that vinegar away, you may want to get a head start on dinner with a simple step out of the way—your salad dressing! Add some olive oil to apple cider vinegar, a little salt and pepper to taste and voilà! You will have a nice homemade vinaigrette to drizzle over your dinner salad—the dinner in which the fruit flies will not be guests! Remember we don't have to let a peewee pesterer stop us from having a bright sunny day. I'm Sunnie. Thanks for tuning in!"

"Cut," Steven calls out then turns directly toward me to say, "You require a lot of editing to get this on by the end of the show. Go back to sounding natural, Sunnie. That's what people want from you."

"Thanks, I'll work on it." *Note to self: Sound natural as you deliver all the lines straight from your mouth that someone else altered and decided would be best, for the ratings! And remember not to take in a deep breath on-air for it is likely that the wardrobe you are clad in would NOT be long enough to cover your panties.*

"Hi! I'm Sunnie, and you're watching the Sunny Side Up segment brought to you today by Add-An-Egg—yummy, tasty egg substitute. A great way to start your day Sunny side up!"

Thank you for tuning in this morning.

Today I have the perfect information you will want to know before the upcoming weekend! Get those picnic baskets ready people; the forecast is wonderful for the fireworks show downtown this weekend." I only hoped that I delivered all the lines to communicate how to prepare a picnic basket with enthusiasm properly. My mind was full of dread of the live taping of my segment on fireworks show night.

A job that used to compliment me, breathing life into every part until it shined like fireworks in the sky, now leaves me feeling as I have inhaled a smoke bomb. Sparklers are so beautiful until they no longer spark—not slow nor fast, just over before you're ready for the darkness to come.

I practically ran out of the room before the word 'cut' was fully pronounced. Mike ran after me, which I'm guessing must have been another obscene showing of my tail as I ran. "Sunnie, are you—" I turn around shocking he and I both.

"Mike, don't ask me if I am okay."

"I was going to ask if you wanted to plan a picnic for the fireworks after the live segment."

"You want to go on a picnic?" I ask.

"Well I just heard of a simple way of how to pack a wonderful picnic, and I felt inspired. And you told me not to ask you if you were okay, so I had to think quickly?"

"So you don't want to pack a wonderful picnic?" I ask with a smile, realizing that I am calming down.

"Well, the station will already be providing the food for us. They do this outing/team building every year, right after the live coverage." Of course, this had been done before sunny girl was on the scene! I feel like the girl of the hour. Mike continues, "We can hang out together with the group…but…if we picnicked there, people would talk."

"Well we wouldn't want people to talk, would we? Plus, what would that do to the ratings?" I remember my irritation.

"What?" Mike sincerely seemed concerned.

"Never mind, I have one more segment until then to get through. Then after the live segment night, I think I feel a 'sick day' or two coming on."

"I know you told me not to ask, but are you okay? Sunnie, if it is about the ratings and about what fans are saying, I could do some little videos of you that you could post. You don't even have to tell

73

anyone it is my work. You can just benefit from the access to the equipment, and the special effects that I can do, so that they can be simple videos, but they won't look homemade. What do you think? I have access to some of the film rooms after hours."

Videos? Make videos of me to boost my ratings? Are you flippin' kidding me? And I don't have to tell anyone it is your work? How totally sweet of you? How's my vibe now, Mikey? "I think I have to pass." I just wanted to get out of there and get some air.

Outside I notice people taking pictures of me as I walk to my car. Lovely. At least I changed out of my barely-cover-my-ass-skirt and gave it back to wardrobe. "Hey Sunnie!" a voice calls out. An old friend comes running with excitement to see me. "So good to see you in person!" She greets me with a hug, and I obviously notice two kids that look just alike are hanging onto her. "These are my boss's kids. I am a nanny now. She works in that big building next to yours. I look for you in this parking lot every day when I deliver the kids to her, but you are never out here. I am so excited to catch you!"

Suddenly none of my day matters, not ratings, not what fans think, just that my friend is so truly happy to see me! "I am so glad you caught me too. Usually, I leave a lot later, but today I am…uhh…getting out early."

"Oh is something wrong?"

"No. no not at all" I lie. "I just have to go let the dog out."

"You have a dog? What kind?" she asks, seeming so happy for me!

"No, I just, uh, let one out for a fan, a friend, I mean. I better go. It is good to see you."

"So great to see you too, Sunnie! You've always made all of us so happy with your comments and your advice and now you—look at you! You have a bigger audience! It must be so great to be doing what you love!" She had no idea how quickly I might trade places with "the nanny" right now!

Logging on, I know it's likely a bad idea, but I do it anyway. Instead of feeling frustrated and misunderstood, this time, I actually feel special, like I could understand, on the slightest level, what my favorite stars go through. I laugh out loud when

I see pictures and the words speculating about my twin toddlers and my nanny. Hysterical! Nothing is ever just about simple Sunnie anymore. Comment after comment about who the father may be. I thought that I had heard it all until I read the next line posted.

Curiousgeorgia: Look closely at today's segment in that tight skirt. Sunnie never had a baby let alone two babies! Amen, Sista! I wish I would stop reading further but of course, I don't! Notice her girlfriend in the picture. SHE had the babies, people!

I wish it upset me more than it did that everyone was jumping in with comments about me having kids with a lesbian lover. To read an equal amount of comments suggesting that I used my babies— possibly fathered by Alec Parker—to get my job, made me laugh. Then I recalled what rumors stemming from either of these scenarios could do for HIS ratings. Sorry Alec, but you can't believe that I would ever want this for myself either.

Who am I? Surely I am not this girl I look like online.

"Hi! I'm Sunnie, and you're watching the Sunny Side Up segment brought to you today by Add-An-Egg—yummy, tasty egg substitute. A great way to start your day sunny side up!" With an exceptional chipper this morning, I deliver my lines.

"Thank you for tuning in this morning. You will be glad you did." Full smile right into the camera. "Today, I will be talking about layers. Yes, Layers! This could be helpful for your weekend plans as well. Now you understand the reason for my casual attire that THE SHOW picked for me for today's segment." I deter from the prompter from time to time, so the crew is not alarmed in any way at this point. "I just love these neutral colored lightweight jackets to add to any outfit after the sun goes down. Sometimes, I even add a pop of color and warmth at the same time by pairing a brightly colored scarf like this. Now I will work a bit in reverse for you to see another option. See here, when I lose the jacket and leave the scarf on, it really fashions-up my t-shirt," removing the scarf taking in a deep breath like here goes this. "Check out this layer without the scarf. You can see exactly how tight my t-shirt is! It's not necessarily too low-cut, but that will come later, in the third minute that I have to educate you people. You get the idea; layers are nice to both cover up or to reveal. It really just depends on what it is that you are selling! You just gotta believe in what you are selling! Whether you want to add a layer and the right jewelry to have your look become the perfect professional-in-an-instant, or maybe you want to subtract a layer for a casual-Moms-group. Perhaps even for a run in the park with your dog. Maybe you get hot, or you just are HOT and want everyone to know it. I like to strip off all my layers and just get real with my audience, natural even," leaning in toward the camera and nodding my head, "Do you want to see Sunnie, without all her layers?" Is everyone on the crew too jaw-droppingly mesmerized to cut this? They just allow me to continue directly into the camera. "Here goes, people." Grabbing near my waist, I begin lifting my tank appearing as if it is the last layer that I could remove.

At least I have learned a camera trick here and there from my experience. The camera and any viewer from a distance sees skin…because THAT is what they want to see. No one calls out 'CUT' as I lift the tank over my head to reveal my two eggs, sunny side up, with a side of bacon in the shape of a smile, placed underneath them. When printing these color pictures from my home computer last night and cutting them out neatly to Velcro directly onto my nude colored cami, I knew for certain I would make a very crafty Mom someday!

"How you like them eggs? My REAL life experience advice for you today viewers—when you add in all the layers that make you, YOU…just make sure that you let no one strip you of your unique sense of humor, spunkiness, and drive that makes you shine." With hands on my hips and complete confidence displaying my eggs, I look directly into the camera.

"I may scramble, but I won't crack. You are watching Sunny Side Up; the segment brought to us by an EGG SUBSTITUTE that I have never tried, yet endorse every day! Yes, you heard that right. My advice: never substitute a fake for the real thing! Thanks for tuning in."

"What?" I yell. "Do your jobs people! Someone say, 'CUT'! That had to be more than 3 minutes! Shouldn't some of you scramble, no pun intended, in a million different directions? Don't just stand there staring at me!" Stopped by the tall, arrogant man blocking the doorway while I attempt to exit, my paper eggs press into his expensive suit. I only wish the egg yolk was real and would slime his Armani as he pulled me in close to whisper something in my ear. Audible for just my ears he admits that he would be fuming if not for being so turned on by my segment. Audible for the staff to hear he finishes his sentence with, "You're FIRED, Sunnie. See me in my office for details."

What details? The line "You're fired" is pretty clear in itself! "Sure thing." Why get upset now, they would be fake tears anyhow. Looking over in the direction of Mike, maybe not all fake. He caught my look and held a stare with an amused smile long enough for me to think that he may just be all that he is cracked up to be.

Walking away from my short, sweet meeting with the Ex-Boss Man, I can hardly believe that I agreed to come to the fireworks still, completing my live segment this weekend in exchange for no mention of the firing in my file. Why not, right? Where could I get a job around here that I wouldn't be a bit type-casted? Maybe I should move far away and start over rather than have people ask why Sunnie doesn't look so sunny anymore. Right or wrong, I still feel happy that I had my chance with stick to my gut and keep it real for those few viewers left that liked me for my sun-shiny ideas. However, FEW may have been the exact wrong word!

The second ring of my phone is the last I hear before picking up to answer. This call comes in before I have proper time to grieve or file a grievance over the firing! I cannot believe what the voice coming from the other end of this phone is offering.

Oh, I don't know, let me think if I might enjoy doing a 5-minute segment on a National Network sponsored by Farm Fresh Egg Company. REAL eggs.

"I accept." Questions? Questions? Of course, I have questions! I will have to relocate, start a new life, do I have questions? "Just one actually. Will boots be provided for the promo video you mentioned on location on the farm? And could I possibly pick those out myself? It would be my first pair."

I love that answer they just gave me! I love this opportunity! Good things come to those with a sunny disposition! Immediately I'm jubilant. I know I can get through this live segment tomorrow as my last commitment in this town. I hope the National Network doesn't see any of my segment recorded today, don't want anyone to think I am a bad egg. Remembering the faces of the crew in the room, every one of them just tuned-in for their own benefit. Not one of them saw anything that they couldn't edit.

They were willing to catch my train wreck on film and then figure out how to edit it back on track. But I pulled it right into the station 'til they all wanted a ride! Well, hop aboard people, because this a runaway train…is not coming back.

Mr. Big Alec Parker's last words play in my head. "Sunnie, after the live segment, who knows? You may feel different come Monday." So let me get this straight, he fires me in front of everyone, but if I am willing to DEAL with all the inappropriateness and sell-out my personality, then he will forgive me and allow me to fake-it-as-directed-per-day while smiling and endorsing fake eggs. I think I got it now!

I'm Sunnie, of Sunny Side Up, and this is not my first breakfast! I would be crazy not to take this opportunity with the National Network. Now that I have had this type of excitement, despite all the drama, I don't know that I could go back to a normal job again. *I have to go for this—a girl's gotta eat!*

Saturday begins lazily, but that will be the opposite of the rest of the day! I lay awake in bed planning what I would wear to the fireworks show if I did get to pick my own clothing for today. Something cute and fun would do. I have Mike's attention already, but I hardly have enough time to explore what his attention could do for me. How silly to spend this much time forming big ideas wondering WHAT IF I could pick this outfit and WHAT IF I had more than one more evening with this man. WHAT IF I just show up and fulfill my commitment to the local network, now there's a grandiose idea!

Exploring all my thoughts and ideas leads me to feel more like Sunnie than I have in months! I had gone in to pitch my sunny idea to that network with such a spunk, didn't flunk, but also didn't anticipate the climate changes I would be in for in my near future. I will be smarter this next time. I will be the kind of sunshine that can shine through the rain. *You can't own the sun, dear Alec! You can enjoy the rays, but it is not something you touch without getting burnt.*

As much as I would love to tell you this in person Mr. A-lec-to-see-your-ratings-soar without-me, I will not mention the relocation until I have done it. I cannot be sure someone wouldn't sabotage my opportunity to keep me here, for the ratings, of course.

Walking through the vacant lot and into that particular wardrobe room for the last time. Greeted by Jaz's smile, that I will miss.

"You get the cutie-patootie halter/shorts jumper!" Jaz says excitedly. I take the hanger from her hand, and smile thank you, a little too choked up to speak without her noticing. "Only one thing bad about jumpers, Sunnie, they are all-on or all-off."

"Jazzy! A fireworks display seems like the kind of place for jumper-all-on!" I sound appalled, but I am not really shocked by her words in the least. Actually, it will help me remember her by, as such a Jaz comment.

"Well, when the 'SUN' goes down, who knows what?" Jaz pantomimes large quote marks in the air when she exaggeratedly says "sun" and I can't help but giggle.

"Jaz, I am going to miss you." I wasn't planning to say it at all, but it felt right.

"Don't be so dramatic Sunnie...only Sunday to get through and then I will see you here on Monday!"

She knows she is funny, but her confidence also says that she thinks she is also right.

"No. Jaz. This is it." I try to sound serious but not dramatic, as I had been accused.

"It's a long day ahead, Sun. Rest assured that Mr. Parker will have every member of staff pulling magic out of their various hats to attempt to get you to stay. Watch out for the trick cameras too!" she laughs again as I turn to go. "By the way, I got all of your wardrobe ready for this coming week. Wow, are you going to look great, Sunnie."

"What? For next week, I won't even—"

"Just following orders!" she smiles as if she really knows a plan about me, even though I am no part of the planning.

I move to the next room, for some more of the same.

"Don't even think of tearing up, doll. It will slow down my process here, your make-up will run, and you will feel very silly come Monday, coming back in here after boohooing about it being your last day. Trust me," Sam rambles to me sitting in the tall chair.

"Who can I trust? Everyone seems to know my future before I agree to it!" I am frustrated that I can't tell, at least Sam, of my plans. Someone nearby could too easily overhear.

"Oh Sunnie, don't be so dramatic. You made your point. Mr. Parker isn't angry with you. If anything...he likes you more than ever. Lips together." *NICE! Wait until it is my turn to speak, then have me put my lips together! Are you kidding me?* "Supposedly, he tells everyone that he got more than he bargained for with you, Sunnie. Hang in there." *Oh yes, of course, he does, I am guessing that he fails to mention what all he gets when no one is looking.* "You're done. Out of my chair...FOR NOW young lady!"

"Goodbye," I choose my words as more permanent ones than a simple "see ya" that I usually deliver. I know exactly what it means.

"Are you ready, Sunnie? Mr. Parker would like to see you in his office before we go," Colleen, just doing her job, says as I pass by her. *Oh golly, I should have figured.*

I am not ready to see him of course.

Are you kidding me in your pale yellow polo against your dark tan skin—the skin that is not all covered in a suit? Wishing that the image I see behind me in my mirror were an illusion rather than Alec suddenly there unannounced, I am undeniably rattled just a bit.

"I know, I look out of place in this office today, more suited for the golf course, huh Sunnie?" *Or under me, while I collect golf balls. WHY did that just pop into my head?* "What are you doing in my dressing room?" I ask as if he doesn't look the way he does right now.

"I told Colleen to have you see me in my office sometime before we leave for the works, but to be honest, Sunnie, I didn't think you would come." *REALLY!* He is a piece of work! Like I am going to fall for that hurt look in his eyes that I may not jump to the orders of my boss-for-one-more-day, as I complete one more obligation to this place.

"Look, it's okay Sunnie, I don't mind coming to you. We have our way of meeting in the middle, you and me. We will get through this, like everything else, Sunnie. Come 'ere."

And that's how I ended up in his arms, smelling his cologne, and melting from the effects. As if it is not strange at all that I have not replied a peep so far, he continues.

"We'll have fun at the works, and then, we'll figure out where the rest of this goes. You are smart, Sunnie and way underestimated—your talent, your enthusiasm, your beauty. I'm on your side, Sunnie. I am going to help you shine, but keep you protected from the world who will try to put out your light," he tells me so effortlessly while rubbing my back with both of his hands.

What he says makes sense, but am I still seeking comfort in the chest of the big bad wolf? Obviously, he knows that I must be drunk on his cologne at this point. He must be assuming that he could slur his crooked words, and they will still speak to me now. I would truly like to think that if I didn't have my relocation opportunity coming up, I would stop him right now. The smart girl that he acknowledged I am would be smart enough to be gone before Monday comes!

For the first time in the one-sided conversation, he tilts my head as if concerned with how I am feeling and waits for me to speak. Here is my chance to speak my mind even if my body is already telling him what he wants to hear.

"I just wanted you to understand me and my sunny personality…I just don't want you to think that this is o—" I sound fifteen rather than a woman in his arms as he cuts me off.

"Oh Sunnie, you don't have to explain anything to me. I am the most misunderstood man on the earth."

I evidently just failed charm school with no degree of integrity to push him away. One soft kiss. I justify that it is one of goodbye.

Forget what I thought of myself, or of a man like this, I am no stronger than all the other girls before me. So much for that light in me shining so uniquely, I am quick to put it out for this—to close my eyes tight and let his smooth ways sweep me off my feet. *Who is the most misunderstood person now? I must misunderstand myself, and live with it.*

I could have enjoyed this sultry kiss more without all of the moral confusion. But that's okay because I get a second try. As I squirm a little at the end of the first kiss to loosen the embrace and free myself of that this-is-wrong feeling, I open my eyes to meet his. His look so intense it paralyzes all but my lips as we both willingly move in on the second desirous kiss—this one more passionate than the first. We should worry that someone would have missed one or both of us and come looking for us. We should gain better control of our sounds or if nothing else, secure and lock the door. Better yet, we should…not kiss...in my dressing room.

This time, when I open my eyes, I stay in his arms but startle from noticing a person looking in on our secret embrace. I will never forget the hurt in the eyes before they quickly shift downward, seemingly embarrassed to be peering through the small opening in the doorway to my dressing room. I cringe, suddenly remembering Colleen also calling him Ale—.

"Wait—Colleen—It's not what you—" I call to the door.

"Let her go," Alec says, not letting go of me.

"Alec, this was a bad idea. You have to go find her and explain."

"Explain what, Sunnie? We are adults. It is none of her business who I kiss in private."

"Alec, c'mon. I saw the look in her eyes. It is obviously her business," I say gently, wanting him to do the right thing, even though I don't know what that is anymore.

"Come 'ere, Sunnie. I want…you now," he says as he kisses my forehead. "She'll be fine. She's a strong woman. Don't underestimate that."

His disregard for this wonderful woman, who has unquestionably been his lover at some point, does not impress me. I push to remove myself from his arrogant aura that had been so appealing just moments ago. I give him a nudge toward the door to leave me.

"You should work things out with her, Alec. I won't be around. Make sure she understands that it was just a...goodbye between us."

"Sunnie, really honey, you are overreacting. Don't talk about goodbyes, especially not now, after we have had this talk and we understand each other a little better," he says before walking out of my dressing room.

I wish I had time to watch you longer and observe you while you have a big cry, I say into the mirror. No time for a gloomy day. I hear all the commotion in the hallway and know that it is time to go.

"Wonderful job, Sunnie!" Steven says enthusiastically with noticeable relief that I stuck to the script this time. "Go on over and get some food and enjoy yourself. I would love to talk to you some more this evening about some ideas I have for your upcoming segments. I'll find you later."

I doubt it! "Sure, thanks, Steven," I say.

"You were awesome on the live segment, Sunnie," Mike says and moves on over to the food table. I know that's my cue to wrap up with everyone congratulating me and make it over to our meeting place to walk to this studio that Mike can get access to for tonight. With difficulty curtailing my excitement, I reply with a thank you to him, just like I had to all of the others.

Finally, I make my way through the crowd, avoiding Alec and anyone else that might hold up our plan. Walking carefully not to twist an ankle in these tall espadrilles, I head straight to our meeting point. I don't even see him anywhere around until he is next to me holding my hand in one of his hands and a picnic bag full of food in the other.

"I tried to grab a variety without advertising that I was packing for two," Mike announces.

"Oh, sure," I reply, still walking hand in hand, so food doesn't matter at all right now.

Mike squeezes my hand that he is holding a bit tighter as he says,"You sure look pretty up close today, Sunnie,"

"Thank you," I say smiling hugely. *Wow, is this what dating him would be like? Cancel my flight!*

"Go down this way, it's a few blocks longer, but will be less crowded. I guess if we are concerned about it, I could let go of your hand," he says laughing, but seems to know that it is true.

"I agree," I say, but do not let go. He doesn't either.

"Well now that we have established that we both know right from wrong here, we will continue walking and doing what feels right, I suppose. I mean technically we left the worksite, right?" Mike says with an amused smile.

"Well, right. We aren't doing anything wrong. No one even seems to be recognizing us together. This probably doesn't happen to you, but lately, it has been hard even to shop through stores because of people coming up to me every minute!" A little embarrassed that I said it out loud, I add, "I didn't mean that the way it sounded."

"No doubt, you are the sunny celebrity around here!" he laughs, teasing me.

"Can we talk about something else, anything else?" I ask.

"Sure, how about Sabbath?" he asks as we continue walking.

"Black Sabbath?" I ask, thinking that maybe I had just heard an old Black Sabbath song coming from a speaker we had passed.

"Ah, an Ozzy fan?" he laughs.

"You're not?" I ask hesitantly. *I thought everyone was.* What are we even talking about?

"Well, of course," he says, smiling at me so long that maybe I should feel uncomfortable, but I'm not. "So whatcha going to do with your Sabbath?" he says, in the same way that he would have said *what's your day like?*

"My Sabbath?"

"Yeah, your day off tomorrow…you know we have this six day work week here this week? I am curious, Sunnie, what do you do to re-center before Monday morning?"

Is this real? Have I met someone who "re-centers" before Monday? Have I met someone who "re-centers" at all? Someone who talks about "re-centering" and looks like this? Oh, I think I will just sleep all day tomorrow so that I don't wake up from this dream!

Tilting his head to look right at me and pull me from my thoughts, he asks, "Still thinking?"

"Oh, yeah, uh…yeah, sorry. I just have a lot of things to do. Yes, I definitely need to, uh, re-center," I laugh a little nervously.

"Oh no, it's okay. I think I caught you off guard. I just like to know how other people, I mean especially someone so positive, like you, re-fuels. It seems it would have to be some Holy Spirit kind of thing, no?" He gives me that same curious smile again.

He sees my Holy Spirit! He sees my Holy Spirit! Holy moly, he sees my Holy Spirit!

"Uh, you…you are like, you are like…uh, and you see…my Holy Spir—" I stutter out then stop babbling to grab his face and press my kiss into him.

"Wow, Sunnie. So the Sabbath, uh, gets you—."

"You get me!" I say, followed by another gentler, longer kiss that I am sure I could do for the rest of time.

"Well, I could stand here kissing you for the duration of the night, Sunnie, but I can't help but notice people taking pictures with their cell phones all around us. Let's just hurry around the corner to the studio I have access to, and then we can pick up where we left off."

We duck in the side entrance with his security clearance pass and make a quick and dedicated effort directly to the studio. It looks so similar to the room where we film the Sunny Side Up segments. He directs me through the door on the far side of the room to yet another beyond it. This room is long and narrow but feels spacious because the entire exterior wall is glass.

"What do you think?"

"What do I think? What do you think I think, Mike? We are overlooking the entire city from up here!"

"You are impressed, and the fireworks haven't even started," Mike says.

"Yes, I am very impressed," I hold a stare as he stares back. I don't want to tell him that I am leaving. I just want to be here with him right now, impressed.

"Are you hungry, yet? We can set up our picnic on this desk by the window. Here, you sit up here on the desk, and I will set everything up for us," Mike says as he lifts me, and my jumper-all-on, up onto the surface. He sets the food in the middle on top of a large, linen, blue and white checkered picnic napkin. "It's not a picnic blanket I realize, but in a pinch, it is not bad, right?"

"Not bad at all," I say smiling, notably impressed again.

"Surprised that you don't recognize it, Sunnie?" he laughs.

"Oh my goodness, Mike, you took that from the set? From my segment, didn't you?" I laugh too.

"Borrowed, Sunnie, I borrowed it from the set! I thought it would be fun to use the whole picnic set actually, but decided it would be way too obvious carrying a picnic basket around, right?"

"Good choice!" I agree.

"I'll be right back. You just enjoy the view," Mike says walking out.

I wonder what he is doing, but not for long because he returns with a vase of yellow and orange flowers, a bottle of chilled wine, and a lit candle for our picnic.

"How did you do all this?"

"Oh don't be so easily amazed, Sunnie. I just thought ahead of time…how a guy like me could pull off a perfect picnic in three simple steps." Mike's smile is so incredible as he turns on the speaker so that we can hear the live broadcast going on outside. "I admit, I came here earlier today to get things set up and in place for our evening to run smoothly."

"Well, perfectly smooth it is! And by the way, I am NOT so easily amazed."

"Oh, but you are, Sunnie! You are. And I don't mean that it in a bad way. You are just…how should I say it? You are just…not jaded. You look at each day new, and you are amazed. People notice that you're different, even Mr.—, well everyone seems to notice, Sunnie," Mike stopped mid-sentence but looked as if he wanted to say more.

"I'm not sure what to say?" I respond.

"Say…that this won't be our last picnic! Here you go," Mike says, handing me a glass of wine to toast. "To beginnings that light up the sky!"

This does not at all seem the right time to mention my job offer and relocation package? I take a sip and swallow hard, swallowing more than the wine.

"Your live segment was flawless this afternoon, Sunnie. I am not sure you realize how good you have become at this. I have never seen such a reaction from Mr. Parker before. No one has. He really wants you…to stay, you know?" Mike says, watching for my reaction.

"Yeah, he made that pretty clear, uh, to me," I stammer out, not sure of how much to say to Mike about Alec. *Why did he have to kiss me? Why did I let him?*

"I am sure he did!"

"He, uh, did. Can we talk about something else?" I ask.

"Why, so that you don't have to admit that he made some moves on you?" he challenges me without the least bit of uneasiness.

"No, not moves, just kissing—a kiss, or two. Whatever, it doesn't matter. It was goodbye." I don't even know why I reacted to Mike questioning me.

"I am glad actually. Now you have had both experiences, Mr. Parker and me."

"That doesn't bother you or give you the wrong idea that I kissed you just hours after I had been kissing our boss?"

"I'm not bothered by it, but I do care about how you feel about it. I assume that you would know the difference between us."

Of course, I know many differences between you two men! "I would rather not kiss and compare, Mike."

"I would rather you not either. You owe me no explanation. All I need to know is that you do know the difference."

"I do know the difference. I just feel strange that we are talking about this."

"Sunnie, I want you to be able to talk to me about anything. I start every weekday with your Three-minute segment of how to have a sunnier day. It is no longer enough. I want that all damn day, every day, Sunnie. I want you. I watch through the camera lens day after day, wanting you. I don't need all of your silly tips to make my day sunnier, I need you, Sunnie," Mike leans in to meet my lips waiting eagerly. The passion behind the kiss is explosive. Could be a scripted scene, it was so systematically effective. Not once in these moments do I think about telling Mike goodbye for my new life to start. Not once, until I hear a vibrating tone coming from his pants.

"Sorry, Sun. I have to take this," Mike says, patting my cheek.

I listen to the one-sided, short conversation without reaction, but I can tell it is something to do with me.

"Apparently, Mr. Parker is asking around if anyone has seen you. He probably wants to try to sneak off to watch 'the works' with you!" Mike says, exaggerating the cheesy way Alec calls the fireworks 'the works' all of the time.

"Oh no. Does he know I am with you?" I ask. I should have no concern since Alec is no longer my boss, nor my problem.

"Not exactly. Tony said that enough of the crew had moved around that he would never assume that we are alone, just the two of us."

"Okay, that's good, I suppose." *Not like he can fire me.* "Does, uh, Tony, and any other of the crew know...about you and me?" I have to ask.

"I called dibs—"

"Dibs?" I cut him off to question his wording.

"Yes, I called dibs on the space here tonight, so yeah, some or most of them know," Mike admits. I don't know whether to be flattered that he had to plan ahead or uncomfortable that others may be in on this. "But if you want to know, I unofficially called dibs on you after one sunny day of you at the station! I am not too proud to admit it, Sunnie, and not embarrassed at all to have chased you for the past couple of months."

"Chased me?" I ask, smiling.

"Yes, the intensity of a chase may seem less due to the ratio of two minutes to every eight-hour shift, but the magnitude building, let's just say, eventually had nowhere else to go," Mike continues, "And anyway, Sunnie, you enjoyed the long chase. It was good for you to keep wondering if you were different than other girls around there. I don't know if you have noticed but I'm a wanted man around the station, you know? You should hear the offers. But you—you Sunnie, you are the one that has everything to offer. Of course, I am going to put forth the effort and clear anyone or anything in my path."

I know that he does not seem to be concerned with Alec in his path, but maybe it is time to tell him about my job offer, that REAL eggs may be a roadblock on the route as well. *How do I begin?*

"So now you know how I feel about things, where were we, before the call?" Mike asks, moving in and touching me so gently, daring my body not to respond.

"Lean closer and I will show you," I say with a very flirty sound. *Not the time to crack an egg, I will tell him later.*

Mike leans in so close toward me; I don't even have to move to meet him. Covered by his mouth and holding on to his arms once again, I know that we should be talking, but having his kisses move across a line of my skin to my shoulder and his hands sliding under my jumper strap, I can't speak. I have waited a long while for this. I made the right choice because the time is hard to come by before his pants are vibrating once again. This time, it's Colleen.

I can hear her voice through the phone, but I cannot tell what she is saying. I mouth "Colleen" to Mike, and he shakes his head to confirm. I pull the phone from him thinking that I would just tell her myself not to worry and for her not to warn Mike away as she had done before—calling him to tell him to stay out of my pockets.

With my jumper-all-on, I put the phone to my ear. Colleen needs to know that he is a perfect gentleman with me. Before I speak, hearing the last thing I thought I would hear, I freeze.

"Mike, we know you are with her. You can call it all off. Mr. Parker says that he has found another way to keep Sunnie here. Mike? Mike? Are you there?" Colleen asks before I end the call.

"I thought you were going to say something to her, not hang up? What was she saying?" Mike asks.

"Well, when I realized that she wasn't positive that you were here with me, why should I confirm it for her?" I reply without revealing what I had heard.

"Well I guess you're right," Mike says, pulling me in for a hug. If this was some kind of game to him, he sure was a good actor. *You never know about the ones behind the camera.*

"Mike, I need you to tell me more what you meant about how you knew that I could figure out the difference between you and Alec? In your opinion, what's the real distinction?"

"Sunnie, I know that you feel different when you're with him. I know his power. I know his tactics. I know how mesmerized Alec is with you and wants to be the one to introduce you to the world like he turned up the last unicorn mermaid. I also know that he will say or do anything in the moment. You felt that. I know you did," Mikes states, in a way that could have been a question.

"Yes, I know," I confirm for him.

"With me, you feel like you want another moment and that I will find moments just for us, not for everyone else. Let me just hold you, Sunnie. Don't feel any pressure from me."

All the right words, smooth man Mike. I rest in his arms with comfort winning over uneasiness. I focus on the tiny red light across the room, as I notice that the sun has gone down outside our window, and we sit atop the enormous wooden desk where we had picnicked, before all of the kissing and all of the interruptions. I choose to believe this man. I want to show him right here on this desk. We can have our moments that he is talking about—getting to know each other, right here, without everyone else. I pull my body up, standing on my knees and look down at his gorgeous face.

"What, Sunnie?" Mike asks, looking up at me.

"You brought me here for a fun picnic in front of the big window, and we have wasted so much of it with the break in calls and talk of what's his name. Now we find out how to brighten the night in a few easy steps," I smile with my eyes and my lips, just like I have been coached to do for the camera. "First, I like to straddle my man like this," I say, pushing Mike back on the desk toward the white board on the wall behind him. "Next, I like to trace my hand on the wall, in case I lose placement at all during the activity." I pick up the green dry erase marker and trace around each of my fingers, giggling since he is nibbling and tickling the skin on the underside of my arm as I reach over him. "Once I have secured my position I lower my body, jumper-all-on until it is pressing into the hot body below me." I can no longer speak or instruct us any further as Mike is responding so intensely well to the brighter day. My hand slides down from its position on the white board to grab the sides of his face and continue the horizontal make-out session.

"Look Sunnie," Mike pulls our faces apart only enough to view the fireworks right outside of our window. Cheek to cheek we watch and breathe together, saying not a word. The most comfortable silence that I have ever heard. "Here, turn over and rest on me so you can see the big finale."

I turn over facing up with my back against his chest. He wraps his arms around me, brushing against my breast, awakening us both from our relaxing, cuddle state. I rest in his arms, watching the fireworks perfectly in sync with the music coming out of the speaker across the room. With his face resting on my shoulder closest to the window to watch the display and his hand caressing my other shoulder without obstruction of the jumper strap, he has pulled down completely out of his way. Mike has lowered it enough that my lace bra, held together by one tiny front-closure clasp, is exposed to the room. I don't mean to, but I keep looking toward the door to make sure no one is entering. The intensity of the music, the explosiveness of the fireworks, and my constant squirming against him seems to be resulting in his further arousal. I feel him breathing heavier on my shoulder, between tasting my skin, his heart beating faster with the build-up of the finale. The final boom sounds off in succession with snap of my bra clasp as well. The lace cups still clinging to each breast, but with it no longer attached in the middle, very little movement will leave me exposed at once. One arch of the back against him and I will pop out instantaneously. Biting my lip, I stifle all but a slight whimpering sound that escapes uncontrollably. All of the room is still and black so that the little red light across the room catches my eye again—the only light in the darkness.

Mike begins aggressively moving his hands up and down my sides when I realize that Jazzy was completely wrong! The jumper that was said to be *all-on* or *all-off* seemed to be at least a third off at this point, exposing my chest to the room and to Mike looking over my shoulder while watching his own hands go for all the newly exposed skin. We are all alone in the dark. What next?

"Mike, what is that red light?" I have to ask. "I'm sorry, it's just that I didn't notice it until it got so dark in here."

"What? I don't know. Just ignore it," he says, pushing my body to turn me over to face him chest to chest, he kisses me harder. I wanted to be right "in the moment" remembering his words about that, and about us. But I also recalled Colleen's words on the phone, telling him that he could call it off. *Call what off?*

"Mike, I'm sorry. It's just…the red light, see, can you check it?"

"Right now, Sunnie? Are you kidding me?" he sounds irritated when he asks. *Way to break the mood!*

"I'm sorry. I have to check," I say as I get off of the desk and go toward the light. "Oh my G—. No! It's a camera. Mike—I think it's ON—"

"Who cares Sunnie" He stands as well, tugs his shirt off over his head, and pulls me back into him.

"I care!" I try to pull away, even though I have never stood next to that sexy a combination of muscles and skin before.

"Can't we figure that part out later, Sun?" He kisses me so hard, lifting me off my feet, turning around, and placing me gently back on the desk.

I wanted to lay back and let go of everything, more than I wanted anything else—anything except the truth.

"Mike, no. I have to go." I desperately hope that he and I both respect the "no" that I say here because I am not sure that I am strong enough to say it twice.

"Sunnie—" I push my fingers over his mouth to stop him, for fear that a plea to stay would come out, instead of the truth. I also fear what the truth may be. He says nothing more and makes no attempt to stop me. At least by this fact, I can always respect that he had regard for my wishes, whether I am right or wrong about any of this.

120

"Hi! I'm Sunnie, and you are watching Sunny Side Up brought to you by Farm Fresh Egg Company, serving all continental states. Now you can enjoy farm fresh egg delivery to your doorstep! No matter where you are watching from this morning, you are never far from the farm!"

"Today I will be talking to you about how to improve 'your norm' with some simple steps. What is 'your norm' and why does it help to determine your happiness or lack thereof? 'Your norm' is what you surround yourself with, and tell yourself is OKAY. For instance, I like to be in the presence of genuinely positive people. Now I am not saying that I only encounter positive people, believe me, I seem to find my fair share of negative ones as well, but I make choices for myself to control my interactions with people that are less than positive. I cannot allow 'my norm' to be sitting around complaining about things that I cannot change. If everyone else around me is complaining or thinking negatively, then I would eventually start to do it too. This is why I cannot allow it to become my norm. A wise man suggested this to me many, many years ago (thanks, Dad!) and I have used it ever since I understood the concept. It applies to everything really: how I talk, who I spend my time with, new habits I take on, and simple decisions about a healthy lifestyle. I can choose 'my norm' as walks in the park over sitting on park benches. If you find yourself in a workplace or social situation where there is negativity or less-than-positive vibes, it is imperative that you do not accept this as the norm for yourself. Let's use the example of a breakroom full of Debbie-downers. You may think that you don't act like them, so, therefore, there is no harm. Not true! Sooner or later you may find yourself grumbling too if you allow yourself to stay. This could, in fact, become 'your norm'. See, when everyone around you is focused on the negative, it can become easy to join in whether you realize it or not. Surround yourself with others who are grateful and that quality could be contagious as well! I don't have any children, yet, but when I do, I plan to pass on this tidbit to help my child find his norm someday.

My advice for you for simple steps toward happiness: Careful what you make 'your norm' today, I hope that it can be a sunny day for all."
"Cut!" I hear, as I look around at a room full of smiling new faces. I think that I could make this my norm!

About the Author

Award-winning fiction author, SC Russell, was born in New York and raised in Ohio. SC currently resides in Cincinnati with her husband and two children with the perk of many grandparents nearby to spoil, enjoy, and build into them!

SC has a passion for writing adult contemporary fiction and children's books as a second career.

She studied in a Psychology Program at Bowling Green State University, and then in a Graduate Program at Xavier University, followed by numerous years of experience in counseling. SC has always concerned herself with how people feel about themselves and their surroundings.

With the desire to be a positive influence to others in person, as well as through her writing, SC will continue to spread an optimistic attitude throughout her message.

SC loves to travel and is most often a destination writer—known for always completing the last writing of each book at an inspirational and peaceful location. SC has an enthusiastic desire to visit and appreciate all National Parks in the USA. She also enjoys: spending time with friends & family, reading as many books as possible, biking tandem with hubby, kayaking on the Great Lakes, swimming in an endless pool while watching the sunrise, and cooking healthy, exciting internationally-themed-meals to ensure that the memories of all the countries visited as a family remains alive in her children forever!

Want MORE?

How about a sneak preview of the next book?

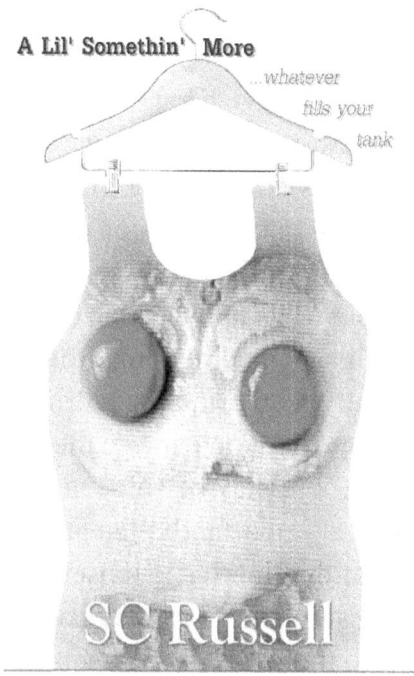

A Lil' Somethin' More
...whatever
fills your
tank

SC Russell

CHAPTER ONE

"Hi, I'm Sunnie, and you are watching Sunny Side Up brought to you by Farm Fresh Egg Company, serving all continental states. Now you can enjoy farm fresh egg delivery to your doorstep! No matter where you are watching from this morning, you are never far from the farm!"

"Today, I will be talking to you about some more ways to improve your health, as part of the BEST YOU series that we have been doing. So if you tuned in last week, you know that we spent a lot of time with segments on shopping for juicing, benefits of juicing, and recipes for juicing. So what happens after juicing? Today, I would like to show you some simple ways to make use of the pulp! Your juicer will separate the juice from the fiber for you. Naturally, you drink the nutritious juice, but did you know that you can use the pulp many ways, as well? There may be some nutrients left in the pulp, but most importantly, the pulp contains practically all of the fiber! The most common uses, well besides tossing it in a chicken coop," I wink, "are adding it to the broth for homemade soups or to the sauce to put over your pasta. Not only can you add fiber to your spaghetti, but you can bake this right into your lasagna or other pasta bakes as well. If you have a little more time, you can add the pulp to your baked goods for extra fiber treats. There are a lot of great recipes online. Last week I tried one for baking raw crackers using my juice pulp. I could have made them in a dehydrator," No I couldn't, my dehydrator is a million miles away, suppose that I'm just lucky to have my juicer here in my new location, "but I just used my oven on the lowest setting. I leave them on for about 12 hours until they were mostly dry, then cut them apart with my kitchen shears before baking them a little longer. If you want to really pulp-out in the kitchen, you could take your homemade crackers to a party with a veggie pulp cream cheese spread to top them! If you think that this all sounds great, but you just don't have time to use the pulp right away, keep in mind that you can store the extra pulp in the freezer until you are ready! Don't worry about losing some of the nutritional value; the fiber will remain! Oh and don't forget to be kind to your dog, pulp dog treats are easy and make a healthy treat for your doggie! I want to add that some veggies are toxic to dogs so please do your homework to avoiding using pulp with those vegetables. I hope that some of these ideas will work for you, so you don't have to throw the pulp to the chickens. Who has chickens these days, when you can get farm fresh eggs delivered to your doorstep? Thank you for watching Sunny Side Up."

"Cut," Robert calls out, "and a nice way to tie the slogan back in, Sunnie. Great work, team."

Sinking into the break room chair, I pull out my veggie pulp cranberry muffin to have with my hot cup of tea. I know that the segment went off well today, but I begin to wonder, as I often do, does anyone even use my tips? I dislike this feeling of doubting my information, and I never actually remember questioning my work back at home. Usually, I felt overly confident, as if anyone who didn't use my tips would be missing out of their chance for a sunny day. Something is really wrong with me. I am starting to doubt the importance of this fiber-packed muffin! I wonder if I could pull off adding pulp to red velvet cupcakes, remembering Mike mentioning one time that they were his favorite.

Taking another bite, I become completely aware of its texture in my mouth. Okay, I am too aware of its texture in my mouth.

"It's that bad, huh?" I hear from an unfamiliar voice pouring coffee by the counter.

"Wha— oh, no, it's fine actually," I say, looking up from my pulp muffin.

"Don't worry, Sunnie, I have no intention of outing you and suggesting that all of your great tips may not always, uh, translate," he smiles. "I'm Gregory," he suddenly reaches across the table to attempt to shake my hand.

Wiping crumbs off first, I finally offer up my hand. "Hi, Gregory. It's, uh, nice to meet you."

"No need to wipe so clean Sunnie, I am hoping to get some of the benefits of the...fiber," says Gregory rather coyly. It is not every day that Sunnie is so openly mocked. Who is this guy? Or, more like, who does this guy think he is?

"Actually, I believe you would have to ingest," I say.

"That's what she said! Ha!" Gregory laughs his way out with his coffee in hand.

Please tell me that did not just happen. I could cry. The only reason I don't is that I have another segment coming up with only a 5-minute make-up touch up. I remember all the times I had sat in the hair and make-up chair back at home with Sam reminding me not to cry and mess up my make-up. What I wouldn't do for someone familiar to walk in the break room, instead of a character like Gregory.

No such luck! I spend the rest of my break listening to two interns flirt in front of me like I am not even there. Only once do they ask me what my pulp muffins taste like, but the question hardly felt sincere. Before I have the chance to answer, the young female intern says that it smells gross from across the room. She continues talking of how she avoids food like that because she's so skinny that she cannot afford the slightest amount of bloating, or it would show on the camera.

"Don't you have another segment recording today, I wouldn't eat that if I were you," the female intern says before they walk out together laughing.

I trash the rest of my muffin. Not exactly because of the comment but because of it no longer tasting appealing. Nothing here seems appealing today. I need my sunny vibe. I cannot think this thought without thinking back to Mike. Why can't there be a Mike at this studio? Is it too much to ask for just one person to notice my color, my vibe, my feel, my...Mike?

I told myself for weeks that I wasn't going to think about Mike or what happened anymore. Thinking about it isn't going to bring the truth, I have moved on, and I am wiser for it. I learned my lesson. The next time a guy at work woos me into a situation where there are secret cameras, and passion, I will know better how to handle it. But that time I walked away. I closed the door, refusing to listen to his explanation for fear he would actually have one. Now I cannot really blame him that I don't have one! There is no explanation really that makes sense.

For me to suspect Mike, or Colleen, or anyone else following Alec's orders, will just leave me feeling paranoid, losing my ability to trust. At this point, I am smarter, but not jaded. It is better this way, coming here, starting all over. It is better! I am Sunnie, and I have something special to bring to any table or desk, I will not doubt myself.

All far away thoughts and self-talks are ended as I hear a voice calling my name. "Sunnie, I was just at hair and make-up, they are ready for you."

"Thanks. I was just about to go down," I say, not admitting to being lost in my thoughts. At least I didn't cry, though.

Walking down to hair and make-up I wonder who I will get today. I do miss Sam and the consistency.

Stepping up to the next available station, I am mineral veiled by a face I do not know.

"You are a new face to me," my friendly attempt to start a little conversation.

"Your face is what matters, not mine," she says and continues to powder me. "All done."

"Thank you. See you later," attempting another friendly exchange.

"Uh-huh," she murmurs.

Not letting it rock me, I pep-talk my way to the studio. I am Sunnie; I belong here. I do add to this place, and to the world for that matter. New outfit from wardrobe, new topic for viewers—it's a new day—in TV world, anyway. Now let me appear well-rested and ready to begin my day, first thing.